This Book Belongs to

_____

AMY KROUSE ROSENTHAL

That's Me Loving You

Illustrations by TEAGAN WHITE

Random House
New York

Text copyright © 2016 by Amy Krouse Rosenthal
Jacket art and interior illustrations copyright © 2016 by Teagan White
All rights reserved. Published in the United States by Random House Children's Books,
a division of Penguin Random House LLC, New York.
Random House and the colophon are registered trademarks of Penguin Random House LLC.

Visit us on the Web! randomhousekids.com
Educators and librarians, for a variety of teaching tools, visit us at RHTeachersLibrarians.com

Library of Congress Cataloging-in-Publication Data is available upon request.

ISBN 978-1-101-93238-4 (trade) — ISBN 978-1-101-93239-1 (lib. bdg.) — ISBN 978-1-101-93240-7 (ebook)

Book design by Martha Rago
MANUFACTURED IN CHINA
10 9 8 7 6 5 4 3 2 1
First Edition

For Jack and Lilly
And always for my three children,
Justin, Miles, and Paris
—A.K.R.

For Dad, who is still singing to me
—T.W.

Wherever you are,
Wherever you go,

Always remember
And always know...

That shimmering star?
That's me winking at you.

That drifting cloud?
That's me thinking of you.

That inviting ocean?
That's me waving at you.

That clap of thunder?
That's me raving about you.

That persistent mosquito?
That's me bugging you.

That butterfly on your shoulder?
That's me hugging you.

That bright sun?
That's me beaming at you.

That beautiful rainbow?
That's me dreaming of you.

That pouring rain?
That's me missing you.

That soft breeze?
That's me kissing you...

That feeling you always have in your heart?
That's me loving you.

Whether together...

Or apart.